Praise for *Eunuch*

'Adeptly using the very particular to get at the achingly universal, Eunuch is a short but striking meditation on difference and belonging. Someone who has always lived in-between will recognise that the stages of dusk are just as real as night and day. Elegant and earthy in turns, evoking whole worlds with deceptively simple words, Carlson's writing recalls the aphoristic poetry of her narrator's era.'
    – Kaisa Saarinen

'In this work, Carlson explores loneliness, humanity, and the individual's relationship with society. Its setting in a distant place and time creates a sense of defamiliarisation yet emphasises the timelessness of the ageing eunuch's thoughts. Carlson's clear, precise language is lyrical, often aphoristic, and the verbal snapshots are like Chinese poems or wood carvings.'
    – Nordic Council Literature Prize

'*Eunuch* recognises the fragility of the happiness of emperors, idle officials, philosophers, and the rich who care only about their riches. Colourful and corporeal,

Eunuch is a continuation of Carlson's deep interest in science and culture – and the way in which an outsider and ageing figure regards the society he both is and isn't part of.'

   – *Kiiltomato*

Kristina Carlson

Eunuch

Translated from the Finnish
by Mikko Alapuro

Lolli Editions
London

Dongjing, capital of China during the Northern Song period, in the year 1120

I

I am a court eunuch, old and retired from service.

I am sitting on a stone bench near the Liang gate of the palace, leaning my back against the wall. It is still warm in September. I can smell the sand and the withering peonies. As I look at my big, fat body on the bench, it looks like a decimated sack of rice, the skin of my stomach sagging. In the bowels of my stomach are raging demons that occasionally force a brimstone-stench through my backside.

I am seventy years old, perhaps a little younger, perhaps a little older. I do not know exactly. I was nine years old when I was operated on and kept at the court. In the court I was given a new name, Wang Wei. It is a fine name, the same as that of a famous poet. Learned men have laughed about this; the ignorant are not even capable of mocking it.

My body may be an old sack, but my wit flows as clear as the water of a mountain brook.

I saw a bird flying against the blue sky. I did not have time to note which bird it was. A crow, perhaps? There are often crows gathering on top of the wall.

I have lived under the reign of five emperors. It is a testimony not only to my advanced age, but also the brevity of the lives of the emperors! My first emperor Renzong died at the age of fifty-two. Yingzong died at thirty-five. Shenzong died at the age of thirty-seven. Zhezong was only twenty-three years old when he died. His doctor was the famous Gen Yu, but even he could not save the emperor. Our current emperor is Huizong, who I believe to be thirty-seven years of age.

What do I know about emperors? I am a lowly eunuch, while the Emperor is a falcon visible only as a tiny dot in the sky.

Because I am old, I have heard a thing or two about emperors. Words which are best not repeated even in one's mind.

The sun warms me. I take a sip of water from a clay bottle and eat a handful of roasted pumpkin seeds. The demons in my stomach start raging when they are idle. I am old, but I do not think about death. I have retired from service and have the freedom to think my own thoughts. Is there anything more one could ask for or receive? Of course there is. Although I am a eunuch, I am not a spiritual monk. I want to drink wine with my friends, I want to eat delicious foods, I want to play dice or *wéiqi* and win copper coins!

I have my own sleeping cubbyhole. Although the window is high, I can climb onto a sturdy chest to look outside. Through the opening I see a plum tree growing on the other side of the paved passageway. It is a great joy! In the winter when the branches are bare, a flock of birds will fill the branches. Sparrows, perhaps? They can be as numerous as the leaves on a tree.

The Old Lady said that reminiscing means stealing from the future. Although I was young at the time, I understood what she meant. Even now I would not care to listen when an old eunuch or retired civil servant starts reminiscing.

There was an elderly lady at court who would not stop talking. In my mind I called her Li Jing, the Silent One. When you said 'rock' to her, she would start talking about the river in her home province that had round rocks on its shore. Young girls would sit on them and sing in the evening. Their song would lure out young men, but the manor house guards would chase them away because the girls were highborn. When the lady heard the word 'silk', her story would start with the mulberry trees in the manor garden, which numbered five hundred or a thousand, and a spinning mill in the valley where the finest silk in the region was spun. If I had the patience to listen to the whole story, it finished with the Emperor wearing a silk coat. The older the lady became, the louder she would reminisce. I felt pity when the listeners fled to other rooms and the lady's mouth was left to play alone like a windchime.

It occurred to me that it is not a good idea to carry your entire life on your tongue.

I do not reminisce out loud but, when I am by myself, people and events pop up in my mind like bubbling river mud.

Once again, a bird's wing slashed through the sky. I like birds. Crows, sparrows, kingfishers, cranes, storks, and falcons, whoever you may be! It delights me when wild birds come to eat grain I have scattered on the ground; even more so when I see the birds fly away in the autumn. Their wings are not clipped like ducks' wings.

There are ten gates around the palace grounds. There are fourteen gates around the city of Dongjing itself. The river Bian flows through the city and, outside the city walls, there is a lake.

It is curious that places like rivers or mountains or forests have names when they have not been built by men. Still, people want to find their way from one place to another, and give names even to landscapes.

I felt like I was being watched. I had just recently finished my service at court.

I looked right and left and glanced over my shoulder but saw no one who was interested in me.

I was sitting in a gazebo with my old eunuch friends. We were playing just for fun, without any stakes, drinking wine and eating nuts. In the middle of it all, I had to turn around again and look over my shoulder. I saw nothing except for the high, decorated column of the gazebo. Behind it there were bamboos, though not a single living creature, not even a sparrow. Still, I had to turn around again a moment later. 'What are you glancing around for? Nothing is hiding behind your back but your past,' said an old, moon-faced eunuch whose name I have forgotten.

It took weeks before I realised where the feeling of being watched came from. It began when I was alone. I had never before been alone in my entire life. I had lived around hundreds or thousands of people ever since they made me a eunuch and I stayed at court.

There are still hundreds or thousands of people around me, but without formal office I am no longer one of them. Now I get to be by myself and think my own thoughts by the wall, in the garden, or on the riverbank. I think my own thoughts, and nobody thinks about me.

During palace rituals the crowd is like a forest that bends in the wind. On a freight trip, I saw a forest far away from here. There were many trees there, growing closely together. I could not see individual trees, but a single, swaying forest. When there are many people, they are a forest, not trees, even though there are different kinds of trees. Thick, thin, young, old, crooked, straight.

When I was suddenly alone, I felt as if an entire forest of people were staring at me.

First it horrified me, as if someone was about to stick a dagger in my back. Such things happened at court. I was not in danger as I was but a lowly eunuch, but high-ranking eunuchs, civil servants and even members of the imperial family could be assassinated.

The most common weapon at court, however, was false speech. *Be wary, my friends, for lying words germinate.*

In reality, nobody talks about me. The ducks, the bamboos, the chrysanthemums, the water of the river; none of it speaks about me. Old eunuch friends might gossip, like myself, but that is only for amusement, as we seek neither power nor wealth.

Seeking power quickly leads to death. Wielding power can lead to death even quicker.

In the evening, when the sun has already set beyond the horizon and long shadows fall in the garden, I walk under the mulberry trees. I am returning from an evening of games with my friends. I have drunk a lot of wine. My head is spinning. Suddenly, a large figure walks towards me. I am frightened. I cannot see the man's face. He is a man, not a eunuch. As he steps closer, I recognise him as a court official I have privately named Silver Tiger. He has thick, grey hair and a chequered grey moustache. We bow and greet each other politely. Without saying a word, he hands me a silk pouch from the folds of his cloak, bows and strides on.

I quickly rush into my sleeping cubbyhole and open the pouch. Money in both notes and coins as well as small jade figurines! I pour the contents of the pouch onto my bed and admire the treasure in the glow of a small oil lamp. I rejoice like a child. I take a couple of jumping steps with my stiff legs. I am too anxious to go to sleep. I have been paid back an old gambling debt I did not believe I would ever receive.

The poor are told to be humble. What else could they be? In my life as a eunuch, I have not been poor like the peasants in the villages, although neither have I been rich like the high-ranking eunuchs.

I have what I need; good, durable clothes, ample food and drink. Nowadays I also have my own abode, a sleeping cubbyhole where I can be by myself. I have a few books, woodcuts, and a brass mirror. I can only wear one set of clothes at a time, just like the rich. My stomach cannot stand large amounts of food or drink. I still drink more wine than I can take. Unexpected wealth is intoxicating, even though I do not know what to do with it. Someone as poor as dirt does not even know how to dream.

On the boundary between drunkenness and sleep I remember, do not reminisce, do not want to remember, and remember.

I am a little boy and I have a brother who is two years younger than me. We are sitting on a riverbank, fishing. Mother shouts from the door and tells us to carry some water instead of sitting there idly. I tell my brother that soon we will bring food to the table and will no longer be idle. We have not caught any fish yet. The water looks green. A dragonfly flutters over the surface. My brother and I get up to carry water from the well. Many days or weeks or months pass. Father says the harvest is ruined; too dry or wet or cold for millet. Father looks angry or sad. Mother looks angry. I am thinking that the weather is not father's fault. My brother and I hide in the shed. Nobody comes looking for us. We start playing a game with small pebbles. When we get hungry, we go home. There is no food on the table. Mother does not serve food. She sits and stares at the wall. Father sits and stares at another wall. Grandmother brings us cold millet porridge but says nothing. We sit in silence until it is pitch dark and everyone goes to bed.

The sounds of different colours. White screeches. Red beats like a drum. Everything is spinning and the world is all mixed up. Is brown the backside of an ox or a horse? Brown hair. I am shaking. In my stomach are either rocks or an emptiness. A man in a grey cape comes and hands me a bowl of rice. My brother gets rice as well. I never see mother and father again. Screeches whiter than white, and black drips. I am being walked along a stone floor, held by the arms as my feet do not support me. I have to walk and walk.

I do not see my brother; I never see him again. After the bandages have been removed from my nethers, I pee, and strange men bow at me. They are satisfied. My life either begins or continues. My brother could not pee; he died. Now that I am no longer a boy and also not a girl, I am a eunuch and get to go to the Imperial court, and mother and father receive money for mc, although not for my brother who died.

> *I am fully awake*
> *and cannot sleep;*
> *it is as if I was filled with dark sorrow.*

When my knees are not aching, I walk outside the city gates. I can smell the manure wafting from the fields far away. I encounter an old peasant pushing a wheelbarrow loaded with swedes, pumpkins, and onions. The man is hunchbacked and sunburned. He says the end of the world is nigh. Year after year the weather has been cold in both summer and winter, and the harvests have been poor. He says that the earth will begin to shake, ice will rain from the sky, and the whole world will freeze.

I recall a drawing of a device by Zhan Heng that measures earthquakes. Cast from bronze, the device looks like a wine jug. Inside is a column that moves. On the top, around the edge of the container, are eight dragon's heads, each with a bronze ball in its mouth. At the bottom sit eight bronze frogs with their wide-open mouths. When the earth shakes, the central column will jolt and one of the dragons will drop a ball inside a frog's mouth. After that, the column will no longer move. The frog with a ball in its mouth will then indicate the direction of the earthquake. I do not understand what use it has! When there is a big earthquake, the dragons will be destroyed as easily as the frogs.

It is comforting for the poor to think that the world will be destroyed all at once. They have nothing to lose. The rich are afraid because they will lose not only their lives, but also their wealth.

I do not worry or grieve. Well, sometimes I do worry and grieve, but I do not think about the end of the world. Is it because my own end is not far off? No, I do not care to think about that.

'Accept your fate,' somebody told me. I don't know who. Perhaps the Master, or the Old Lady?

I do not understand what this imperative means. Am I supposed to bow my head for the swordsman to chop it off? According to this wisdom, I would have to accept what has already been determined, because nothing else is possible. What sense does that make?

I have never had strength or power, but I am still not a goat or a ploughing ox! In my home village, my parents had to bow in the face of poverty, although that was not about surrendering to fate, but the fault of poor harvests. I refuse to accept the idea that things could not have been different. My parents sold myself and my brother as eunuchs because we were poor, and I also had five sisters. Necessity is not the same thing as fate, or does the imperative claim otherwise? Who determines fate? The heavens? The Emperor? Fate is often decided by the local officials and major landowners, lords of the manor. It is not fate; it is necessity. I cannot think any further than that. I am an old, stupid eunuch.

After the operation, after I had successfully peed and received a name, I was sent to work in the palace kitchen. Steam and burning grease. I did not stay in the kitchen for long, for I was a handsome child. I had thick, dark hair, round limbs and a cheerful face. When I look at myself in the mirror now, it is hard to imagine, let alone remember. I was then sent to work in the palace harem.

I was both confused and enchanted. Women of all ages, some finely dressed, others in thin underrobes. I swept the floors and dusted the tables, shelves, and sculptures. The women would comb their hair, laugh and chat, and the younger ones would run around from room to room, like children. Their faces were as pale as the moon. In the kitchen I had only seen crude men's faces; moustache hairs and skin red from heat. The women's rooms smelled of jasmine and peonies. I was amazed at how different women were from men; I liked women more than men. In the eyes of women and men, I myself shall never be either because I am a eunuch. I started off as just a child, but within my earliest years, I was more and more clearly a eunuch.

When I wiped objects with my duster, I tarried to hear what the women were talking about. They chirped quickly, like birds. I could not make out the words. I was not trying to spy on anyone. Only much, much later did I realise that it is something eunuchs also do; listen, tell, and get paid for it. The court is a pot where gossip boils, and not all talk is innocent chatter but may lead to assassinations and executions.

When I was little, young women touched, stroked and tickled me as if I were a kitten. I was not a man or even a boy. They spoke to me in the same high-pitched voice as they would to a pet, tilting their heads and giving me little kisses. This did not last very long. I grew in height, gained weight and became clumsy. I began to look like a eunuch.

There was a lot of thick fat around my waist that my bellybutton would sink into. My beard did not grow, and my face was as round and shiny as a baby's backside.

I was no longer a toy or a pet. Still, I was not treated badly, for I was well-mannered and friendly. Not all eunuchs are. Many of them serve in the army or as palace guards. Perhaps not all men lose their personality when their genitals are cut off.

I was surprised when I was addressed in the harem by a lady with a broad face and stocky body. She was neither beautiful nor young. She stopped my broom with her silk shoe and said: 'Look here!' I stared at the floor. I did not understand what she meant, though she was not speaking a foreign tongue. 'Look at me, eunuch!' she said. In fright, I raised my chin and looked at the lady. I was surprised, because despite her stern tone, the look on her face was gentle. I can no longer remember what she then said or what I replied. I probably said nothing. She then told me to call her the Old Lady. She was not like Madame Liu or Madame Gao, who acted as regents. Because of all the paranoia at court she told me to call her the Old Lady, and so I have always done.

One of the very things she taught me was that names should not be used at court. She explained that if you tell Number One what Number Three said about Number Two, and Number Two finds out, everyone will ask who said what, and when they have a falling out, you will be the one who gets the blame. 'Then they will all agree to cleave you in half at the waist, and I think your bellybutton will end up in the lower half because you are fat,' the lady told me. I tried to follow her advice, but as I have grown older, in my mind, I have begun to slip.

The Old Lady was my protector and mentor. The other young eunuchs used to laugh at the way I followed her around like a duckling. They even mockingly called me Duck, because I had a long back and a heavy stomach, and I waddled when I walked. My friend Wong Wu says that the Old Lady still talks to me, even though she died a long time ago. Which is true.

The Old Lady told me: 'You are too lazy to be good, and not cunning enough to be evil.'

She said: 'Unfinished work leaves an ache in the bones.' She encouraged me to learn to read and write and eventually read books that would help me pass the civil service examination. I read the Book of Songs and the Master's works; I still have the books but never took the examination. Perhaps I was indeed too lazy to be good, if this is what the lady meant when she said that. I did not advance in my career; I did not become the sort of high-ranking official who retires with land and manor houses, living a life of luxury.

When I studied as much as I could between cleaning and other chores, many of the other eunuchs would mock me. They said that the Old Lady was a fountain of wisdom, but that I was a filthy cesspool of knowledge. This made me feel sad. I did not understand that one will no longer have friends in the outer circle of power if they think one is seeking to enter the inner circle.

In reality, many other eunuchs tried to study too, because they hungered for power and wealth. Some did pass the civil service examination, and some of those were given important administrative tasks. As they rose up in the hierarchy, they became as important as men. They forgot their old acquaintances, the other eunuchs. Face southwards, like the Emperor!

Although us eunuchs at court are so populous that we are like a realm within a realm, we lack power. We were – are – servants, and power is everything.

Emptying the emperor's chamber pot is one eunuch's job. I wonder what sort of diploma he has that qualifies him for the job. At least he gets to see a unique depiction of the emperor: the turds floating in the pot.

There was a woman in the harem who was no longer young and who liked to look at her reflection in the mirror all day long. She had beautiful almond eyes and a red, rosebud mouth. I never saw her smile or laugh; she always wore the face that she put on in front of the mirror. A year passed; many years passed. Still she sat in front of the mirror staring at herself and still she had almond eyes and a rosebud mouth. I wondered if she had ever smiled or laughed. Perhaps not, since she only ever conversed with her reflection.

There were women in the harem, wives of the Emperor who did not give birth to children. Perhaps once upon a time such women were slain or returned to the homes of their fathers. I do not know. Many of the women behaved girlishly and recklessly because they did not have children. Just as many lost weight and mourned in the corners. They did not even comb their hair. I felt great pity for them. Although my body is more like that of a man than a woman, perhaps I have the mind of a woman.

The Old Lady was not always old, and not always a lady. I heard that her father had been a major landowner and that she grew up in an impressive palace surrounded by a large garden. It had a pond, a waterfall and a mound built out of rocks. 'I was a light, happy, agile girl, but I was not beautiful,' she told me. Her parents were worried that their daughter would be unable to enter into a good marriage. She was not; she became the Emperor's wife. She gave birth to a son who died one month old. She never had other children, but the Emperor liked her, and the lady stayed at court during the reigns of several other emperors. She did not hold any power, unlike Emperor Zhedong's mother Gao, who ruled in her son's stead.

One thin, pale-faced girl sat all day along the wall of the room playing the lute. She never smiled. She never had fun with the other women. I never even saw her eat. A year or two went by, and I learned that the thin lute player had died. It made me sad. She always used to play as if she was playing at her own funeral.

It is nice to watch the ducks at the pond. They are not graceful like swallows or cranes, or majestic like eagles and falcons. They are homely. As they bustle around, they look like busy country women. The ducks in the pond cannot fly because their wings have been clipped. The ducks are white or brown, almost black or chequered. When I look at a duck from the side, it looks like it is smiling. As it dives, the duck's tail and yellowish-orange webbed feet remain above the surface.

I like duck at the dinner table, too.

A chequered brown duck is chasing a white one along the lawn and pecking at its tail feathers. They both dive in the pond, and water splashes as they attack each other. Soon the water grows still. The chequered duck swims to the left, the white duck to the right. Their feathers are left floating in the water, the aftermath of a battle.

In the harem I was the women's favourite, but this meant that I also had enemies in court. I do not know who they were. Why else would they have sent me to war?

I travelled with Emperor Shenzong's troops to fight a war at the barbarian frontier.

This was one of the many border skirmishes before the Great War which our forces lost.

I was not one of the warriors, of course, but looked after food, drink, and other necessities with the other eunuchs. As I was already fat at the time, I was made to sit on a cart next to the millet sacks. The horsemen believed that no horse would be able to carry me.

While the warriors fought, I was forced to spend time in a village that belonged to our enemies.

In the yards and fields, I saw old men, women of all ages, and children. Their faces and clothing looked different from ours, but the chores they did were familiar. They carried water and gathered firewood. Old men sat by the walls of houses the same way I sit against the city wall. Little boys crouched by the brook, trying to catch fish with their bare hands. They were foreign people, so I did not know whether their faces were fearful, resigned or the same as always. I did not hear what they said to one another. They spoke little, and even if I had heard, I would not have understood as they spoke a foreign language.

But I understood what happened when a woman ran from the yard and grabbed a boy who had jumped into the water by his ear. The boy wriggled like a frog. I saw an old man trip and fall while carrying two buckets of water on a pole. The water splashed onto the ground, and he raised his thin arms towards the sky and cried out. I thought how the soldiers never see this life, as they are always fighting, riding in a cloud of dust and killing the villagers.

On the battlefield, the enemy is cloven in half at the torso. This is also done in our land when a person has committed a crime against the Empire. The top and bottom half of the body; the parts of a human. I have had only a part of my bottom half cut off, not with a scimitar but a thin-bladed knife. And I am still alive and was allowed to keep my head.

The village was burned after the fighting was over. The ruins were smouldering and the body of a child lay on the yard, stomach ripped open. Leaning against a burnt wall was a charred man who had lost his head.

The general came to our field kitchen for a bowl of chicken soup garnished with onion. The look on his face was the same as always, and he was careful not to wet his moustache while eating his soup. I felt cold and sick. I wondered if fighting and killing was all in a day's work, after which a man goes home to his wife and children, drinks a glass of wine and plucks a lute.

After the campaign I was ill. Still I was ordered to stand guard by the wall with a scimitar at my waist, even though I had never wielded a blade greater than a kitchen knife.

I was standing guard when a Great Wise Man was brought to the court from the West. A crowd of a thousand courtiers in fine colourful silk and ornate headgear gathered around to listen. The Wise Man was paid for his words in grain, silk, jade, and gold. The Wise Man bowed. The courtiers lifted their faces towards him, and everyone bowed. The hot sun beat down from above and yellow dust was swirling in the air from tens of thousands of footsteps. I was standing too far away to hear the words of wisdom. I thought that if I knew how to use a scimitar, I could have cut the speaker into two pieces of flesh. Which half would have held the wisdom? Men like to suggest to eunuchs that intelligence and wisdom reside in the lower half of the body.

Much later I asked the Old Lady what the Wise Man had said. She shook her head. She could not remember. She said that rats and vermin and speakers of wisdom breed during years of famine and border skirmishes.

I was found worthless both in the field of battle and as a guard when I tripped over my scimitar and split my little toe. I don't know what my tormentors intended, but I was happy to get back to the women's chambers. I have not spent my whole life sweeping floors or dusting, though; over the years I was given more important tasks.

I was made an assistant of the harem women's wardrobe. Dresses, ribbons, and buckles needed sorting, storing, cleaning, and repairing. Oh, the colours, the scents, and the touch of silk! I felt like I was archiving flower petals. Because I could read and had a good head for numbers, I was made to keep a record, first of clothing, and later, of other supplies at the harem as well: cloth, jewellery, decorative objects, furniture, plants, tableware, tea. But at that time, the only thing I sensed in the corner where I worked were the scents of paper and inkstick.

The rich cannot retain their riches unless a record is kept of everything. If a poor person suddenly becomes rich, they will spend the money on fleeting desires. I too am a poor person who dances for a handful of coins!

For the last years of my working life, I returned to the wardrobe. I was once again near the women of the court and the loveliness of flowers. I had the power to choose between two or three silks when new clothes were sewn.

I do not know what I know, but I know that I do not know what it is like to be a man or a woman. It says in the Book of Songs: *There are two who cannot be taught or controlled – a woman and a eunuch.*

I do not understand. Are a woman and a eunuch more alike than a man and a eunuch? Are a woman and a eunuch both stupid and stubborn, and lesser than men?

I can say that I love peonies or ducks or copper coins. I can even say that I love my best friend Wong Wu, but I do not know how it feels when a man and a woman love one another.

Yin and yang are the shady and sunny slopes of a mountain. Yin stands for femininity, yang for masculinity. In the symbol, shadow and light are wrapped together into a circle. Where do we eunuchs belong? Perhaps we are the white dot in the black, and the black dot in the white of the symbol?

On a bench by the water lily pond sits a woman reading a book. She does not notice me as I walk down the gravel path. I walk to the Zheng Gate. Behind the gate stands an old man with a bundle on his crooked back. His hair is tangled and he is wearing tattered, dirty clothes. He is talking loudly and shaking his head. I cannot understand what he says. He is either from a foreign land or a madman. Because he frightens me, I wave my arms to shoo him away. He will not budge. After a while I can see that the man is blind. His eyes are as white as those of a cooked fish. Pity floods into my mind. I turn away. I am not poor, blind, or mad.

As I sit leaning on the wall, a man with two children arrives at the courtyard. Judging by his clothes, the father is a high-ranking official. They are running around; the man is pretending to chase his little boy and girl like a horned bull. He has turned his palms against his forehead with his fingers stretched out. The children are screaming with terror and joy. I smile. It is rare for a father to play with his children; as rare as a donkey pushing a cart backwards.

What if a child had crawled out into the world from my fat stomach! A girl; it would have been a girl, even though the Book of Songs says that a boy gets to play with jade figurines, but a girl with pieces of brick.

In the villages, there are children born who do not seem obviously girl or boy. They are usually killed right away. Bodily defects are shunned in our realm: harelips, crossed eyes, clubfeet, hunchbacks. We eunuchs are incomplete, because we are neither men nor women, but we have been operated to be this way. On purpose, for money, to be fit for service.

Long Fan looks like a scalded pig. His skin is light and hairless. He does not even have eyebrows or lashes. His head is shiny, conical, and spotted like a bird's egg.

He is a eunuch. He says he was born without hair, which confused and terrified not only his parents, but the entire village as well. The villagers thought the child would not survive, but Long Fan grew up to be a spry and plump boy. Without hair. His parents took him to a trader when he was ten years old. He was accepted precisely because he was odd. The women at court found him delightful. Like a giant baby, smooth and soft.

How long did the women's admiration last? For a year, perhaps two? Then it was time for something new! Long Fan was transferred to the kitchen but, because he learned to read, write, and count, he spent decades working in the palace archives.

The deformed, the ugly, the crippled all delight the court, even though anomalies are usually looked down upon in our realm. Children are slain if they are defective, but the court is amused by a dwarf whose stomach starts from underneath his chin, a thin lanky fellow with cabbage leaf ears, or a woman whose nose touches her lower lip.

In the evening I lie on my bed and watch the torch-light reflecting from the brass mirror.

Wong Wu and I once travelled in the entourage of a high-ranking official on a visit to his home province. We eunuchs were responsible for foodstuffs and gifts. The midwinterly weather was cold. The carriage rocked because the mud of the road had frozen into hard, deep grooves. Snowflakes began to fall from the black sky. It looked as if the stars were floating down to the ground. My head was freezing, my hands and feet were freezing, and I was also terribly hungry.

When we finally arrived, the carriages of the dignitaries continued on to the manor, but we servants were left at an inn inside the city walls. In the warmth of the coal-heated pots, I began to thaw. Hot soup, rice, chicken, and fried vegetables were brought to the tables. Even the thick, yellow wine had been heated. I, Wong Wu, and the others grew cheerful. The people at the inn treated us with respect because they knew we were part of a prestigious entourage.

After we had eaten, I suddenly noticed a strange creature in the corner. She was a very old woman, as thin and dry as an insect, but her grey hair was thick. It looked as if a fly was wearing a hat. She kept staring expressionlessly. I realised that she was blind. The woman who kept the inn noticed me watching the old lady in the corner. 'She cannot see with her eyes, but she can see the future,' the innkeeper said. 'Would you like her to tell your fortune?'

'No, no,' I said, but Wong Wu had had more wine than I and become bold. He asked for a fortune-telling.

Wong Wu picked up a low stool from the floor and stepped across the room to sit in front of the old woman. His back covered my view, so I could not see whether she used magical instruments or how she did her fortune-telling. The innkeeper poured me more wine. By the pleased look on her face, I gathered that Wong Wu had slipped a payment for the fortune-telling into her hand. I had barely had time to drink the wine before my friend returned to the table. His round-cheeked eunuch's face shone in the light of the lanterns. It looked like Wong Wu was about to choke, and I was frightened. We were only around thirty years of age; surely his time had not yet come! What if he had a stroke and died instantly? The innkeeper hurried to fill our wine goblets. 'Did you hear your fortune?' I asked anxiously. Wong Wu burst into laughter, spattering wine all around. 'I did! I shall pass the civil service examination, advance in status, and marry the governor's daughter, and we shall have five sons who will all be handsome and wise. We shall live in a manor house with a koi pond in the garden. We shall live a good, long life.' I laughed too, and said: 'Since things are going to go so well, I assume you are not going to ask for your money back.'

I drift along the river Bian, lying on top of old sacks at the bottom of a boat. I had been sitting by the river on a pier and a fisherman asked me to join him. He said we were related. I felt like smiling. Am I even related to myself? I agreed, of course. Since it is autumn and a grey day, the weather is cold, but it feels nice behind the cover of the boat's sides.

The wind above the river smells of water, and the boat smells of fish. As I peer above the side, I see other fishermen's boats and large ships carrying goods from one port to another. I cannot hear people's voices, but see them on the waterfront, scurrying around like ants. There are so many goods that we need! Fish and rice and millet and tea and wine, of course, but the large ships also carry fine table sets, lotus-shaped bowls, bronze goblets, silken cloth, small sculptures, and small painted boxes that people need or think they need. With all this the human ants toil like there is no tomorrow.

The map of the city fascinates me like a poem. The name of the river is Bian, and it curls into the depths of the city, only to be free again outside the gates. The wall of the inner city has ten gates. When I leave the city limits, I usually pass through the Liang gate, because it is the shortest way to the lake along the river. Still, the trip is so long and my knees ache so much that nowadays I need a lift.

The city of Dongjing itself is unfamiliar to me, even frightening. I have lived my whole life inside the palace walls. When I leave the palace grounds, I try to find a short route to the riverside or the meadow. Our present Emperor Huizong has constructed a wonderful garden and an astonishingly high mountain out of loose stones in the city! I have not seen it, though. There are fine restaurants in the city that make delicious food catered to southern tastes. I have never tasted it! There are thousands of people in the city: footmen and people carried in sedan chairs; traders, craftsmen, and beggars; sales carts moving along alleyways, bathhouses, workshops; buzzing of speech, cries, squeaking of wheels, clattering, colours, smells.

There is too much of everything.

I drift, and thinking about thinking is a pastime.

Many think that the world has been divided in two. There is day and night, light and darkness, hard and soft, man and woman. This is what their reason tells them, even though they know that there is also dusk, and that water is able to flow and steam and freeze.

The river runs, it is not like a road people travel along. On any sunny day the surface of the river was shiny, soft silk. It shone in the sun, and in the narrow passage along the riverbed, the trees were reflected on the surface of the water. Even the clouds were sailing along the water. Suddenly, ripples underneath broke the still surface. I felt as if there was a large animal hiding in the bottom. A dragon.

I was not thinking. I remembered; I was a little boy.

Rivers run towards a larger body of water, the sea. I have never seen the sea. Seas join to other seas.

I am lying in the bottom of the boat. The fisherman does not speak. That is good. Suddenly, I smell the stink of the pigsty located along the river. The smell of pigs is awful, and also wonderful. People smell a lot worse. I love the smell of pigs and their taste when the meat is sizzling on a fire or floating in soup along with onions. I love the humble looks of pigs, their moist, trusting snouts and white-lashed, innocent eyes.

I would not eat people. The nastiness of people would ruin the taste of the meat.

Thinking about thinking also means thinking about what I once thought, if I ever thought at all. If I could even remember.

The boat trip was exhausting, even though the river carried me. I shall rest on my bed before I go to play dice with my old eunuch friends.

My body feels heavy.

Although the skin on my stomach is wrinkled, there is still so much fat in me that my bones click and rattle when I turn. My buttocks ache. Sometimes a pain shoots through my shins like a flash of lightning. I try to ease it by thinking about pleasant things. I think about little green frogs hopping in the wet hay of the river delta. Their backs are glistening in the sun. Suddenly, a stork flies into the reeds, stretches out its beak, and grabs a frog. I become sad again and feel the pain even in the soles of my feet.

The rising moon at the window looks like a toenail.

A friend of mine wonders how the world was born and how it works. I do not think such great thoughts.

I walk through the Liang gate into the city and continue on my way towards the palace. On a stone bench by the gate sits an old woman with a jagged chin whose job is to sweep the paths. She never greets me, though we see each other often. She never greets anybody. She will sweep and smooth the gravel path, and when somebody leaves footprints on it, she will rush over with her broomstick and start angrily dusting up the gravel. She cannot stand flowers, such as peonies and chrysanthemums, because flowers shed their petals. When the wind has tossed some on the gravel, she picks up the petals one by one.

I am a good-natured person, but sometimes an evil thought rises up like a sour belch: I feel like kicking the gate warden woman in her skinny buttocks! Because she is grumpy, hostile, and secretly resentful. I probably would not even be able to kick. My knee hurts too much. I swallow the bile inside my mouth.

We eunuchs are fat, soft, and round, and many think that fatness is a sign of friendliness. Still, we come in as many forms as men and women. Rough, stupid, cunning, lazy, cruel, greedy, wise, gentle; anything you can find in the world.

The Old Lady said to me: 'You are like a child.' She did not mean that I was cute; she was referring to my trusting nature. I think well of people. Usually. In her opinion, there was no reason to. I thought she was wrong.

43

My friend Wong Wu said that lazy people talk a lot because they are unwilling to act, that is, to get anything done. I was afraid that he was talking about me, because I used to talk a lot when I was young. No, he meant officials, ministers, those in power who design wonderful roads, dams, walls, bridges, and cities that are never completed. Those in power stay in power on the strength of spoken words. Because building a wall, dam or bridge takes decades, the official will die whether the project is completed or not. No one will ever catch him for lying. But his pay – the land, manor, and gold – will pass on to his next of kin. This is how the realm works. As my great namesake Wang Wei wrote: *I can still hear the pines sighing in sorrow, or perhaps it is the moaning of a minister.*

I talk and think to myself; no one can hear.

In this Empire it is dangerous to think and speak.

My friend Zhang Li was a wise man. He was a man, not a eunuch. He had a goatee that fluttered when he spoke. He knew much about everything. I am not uneducated myself, but Zhang Li was without equal. He could quote the words of the Book of Songs or the teachings of the Master at any time but had also studied astronomy and mathematics. I was surprised when he claimed that the world was born after Nagua had rolled in the mud, or out of the egg of the giant Pangu. He began to speak this way when the reign of a new Emperor began. Because I was a trusting person, I did not understand. Zhang Li started using knowledge to please those in power. He advanced in his career. He changed his cosmology many times. I had not realised that he was a social climber who deep inside was greedy and hated the world. 'A snake,' said Wong Wu.

Master Kong makes me nervous, because he is respected in the realm, but I do not like him. I read his Analects for the civil service examination. The Master has said: *Worry not that you have no status but about what it takes to gain status. Worry not that you are unknown but seek that which shall make you known.*

I could not understand. Was I supposed to walk around the palace hallways and garden plazas talking about and praising myself? That is precisely what many do, however.

The Master's teachings set strict limits for the behaviour of an individual person and the state and the use of power. He commands that: *A gentleman shall not decorate himself in bluish or reddish violet or wear crimson or purple everyday clothing.*

45

It is said that the Master's teachings are gaining an ever stronger hold on our land's government. What do I know? I am not a politician, just a stupid eunuch.

When the Master describes his own life, he says that: *At the age of seventy I shall follow the desires of my heart without breaking the boundaries of conventionality.*

I am in my seventies! I want to follow the desires of my heart and break the boundaries of conventionality!

Conventionality forces life to go on the same way it supposedly always has. Yan Yan taught me that if the shoes chafe your feet, walk barefoot.

I think about my thoughts about thoughts.

As young eunuchs we rebelled by drinking a lot of wine. It did not make us wise or poetic, though we thought otherwise. No, we staggered and stammered and vomited into the bamboo bushes. The shade of the bushes was black as ink, but our words of wisdom were never written down.

I sat at the gambling table and looked at faces I had known for decades. I drank wine and ate nuts and dried plums. As the evening grew dark and the lanterns were lit, the faces looked like masks in the light and shadows.

Suddenly Ji Nin jumped up from the table. He began to recite a poem that was reminiscent of the Book of Songs, but I knew that was not where the poem came from. I and my gambling companions looked at Ji Nin in amazement. He had always been a quiet eunuch.

Ji Nin recited the poem and went on and on, and from what I could understand, the poem was not bad, though not up to the poetry of the masters. I took a moment before I realised that the poem he recited had not been written; the verses were born in his head and fell from his lips that very same moment. Ji Nin's head worked like a waterwheel, that operates machinery, and his machinery was churning out poems in a ceaseless flow.

It has been weeks and months since Ji Nin started writing poetry. He has not stopped. Mostly he recites, but someone says he also writes. If he writes even nearly as much as he recites, even the sheets of paper the court reserves for wiping their backsides will not be enough.

Madness is different from other diseases: one gets used to it. Both the madman himself and other people. Ji Nin used to be a quiet eunuch; now he is a eunuch who writes poems. Many avoid him, but he is of no harm to anyone, though he is often tedious. I have

47

sat beside Ji Nin and listened to his poetry at the back of the Northern Jinglong gate where it is quiet.

Wong Wu is my oldest friend. And my best friend. At times, he has even been my only friend.

After I had been operated and I had peed and was able to walk, I was put to work in the palace kitchen. I carried onions and beetroots and herbs from a cool storeroom. I was not yet strong enough to carry heavy sacks of millet and rice. The cook's assistant Yu Bo ordered me around. He was a skinny, sweaty man. Once, he told me to fetch a basket of onions. The storeroom smelled of earth and vegetables. As I was lifting the bamboo basket, I saw a pair of eyes glowing in the dim corner of the storeroom. I was so frightened that the basket fell from my hands and the onions rolled across the floor. A rat! I was scared of rats. I squeaked like a rat myself. Even though I feared the wrath of Yu Bo, I was too afraid to pick up the onions. I was too afraid to move. I heard a shrill sound that was not a rat, but a child. A boy was huddled in the corner. I became twice as frightened. I turned on my heels, left the onions on the floor and ran to the kitchen. I pulled Yu Bo by the sleeve, even though it was inappropriate. I whispered to him what I had seen in the storeroom. I thought he would call the palace guard eunuchs to get rid of the rat that was not a rat, but Yu Bo said, 'show me!' As we stood in the storeroom, the eyes were not in the corner where I had seen them. We remained silent and unmoving, and then Yu Bo noticed the eyes under the lowest shelf at floor level. He whispered in a dialect I could not understand. A child crawled out to the hallway. He was my age or older. I realised that he had not been operated; he was a real boy.

In our state, mercy is a weakness, not a virtue. Was Yu Bo weak because he showed mercy to a boy who was his distant relative from a far-away province? He had the boy operated, the boy survived, was named Wong Wu and got to work in the kitchen. His nickname was Rat, just like my nickname is Duck.

Wong Wu and I once wondered if he could have stayed at court and pretended to be a eunuch. No one ever sees us naked. There are eunuchs who still have their penises. Some eunuchs were known to have been the lovers of Empresses!

Wong Wu is my best friend, but there are others. They tell me things they do not tell anybody else, warning me not to tell anybody. I will not tell, which is a precious promise, because one of the most valuable currencies in court is gossip. My friends will remember me when things are bad for them or something wonderful has happened. They want to tell me everything. When life runs along its usual course, they will not remember me.

We are walking along the riverbank, Wong Wu and me. There is a breath of autumn in the air. Seasons pass by surreptitiously. I look at the sky but cannot see the migrating birds. At the edge of the sky's blue dome, a grey cloud is drifting. There is a smell of the water, the mud on the beach and brown reeds. We walk slowly, the way two old people do. Wong Wu has always been skinnier than I. He worked in the kitchen all his life and was promoted to become a respected cook. High-born guests from far-away places came to taste his food.

In shady spots the river water gleams dark yellow. We sit down in the hay on the riverbank. A puff of insects rises up from its strands. We have fried rice cakes and water in a bottle. We eat and drink and lie down. I listen to sounds that are mere whispers: the rush of water, the rustle of the wind in the reeds, the buzz of a flying insect. I fall asleep.

I wake up with a start. I sit up in horror. I turn my head around and look in every direction but can see nothing but Wong Wu sleeping with his mouth open. I notice that he has a lot of teeth missing. I do not know whether I have been awoken by danger or had a bad dream. As my head clears, I am ashamed of my panic. I stand up and shake dirt off my clothes. Wong Wu wakes up suddenly and springs up. 'What is the matter?' he asks. 'Nothing,' I reply, and we continue on our way. I feel as if something had extinguished the brightness of the day. I do not know what.

II

Where is my pao? A *pao* is container with a lid where my testicles and penis are kept. A eunuch cannot be buried without a *pao*. Why did this question spring to my mind?

Wong Wu comforted me, telling me that a *pao* can be bought if the original cannot be found. He said it is not something I should worry about. He is right, of course, but still. If I have to be buried whole for the afterlife, what will happen when another eunuch's genitals are buried with me? In any case, I suppose a little boy's jewels are like dried wood ears, the fungus that grows on trees. Or were the organs preserved in a fluid, such as oil? I do not know. Since I do not even believe in the afterlife, I worry for no reason.

They say that if a eunuch is buried without a *pao*, he will be reborn as a woman. Would that be a bad thing?

Demons have been raging madly inside my stomach. Because of this I went to see a doctor.

I remember my operation into a eunuch, though only as sounds and flashes of light. I have feared doctors my entire life ever since. My doctor was a tall man with a wrinkled face and a thick, grey moustache. We greeted each other politely, but after that he did not speak a word. It was hard for me to talk about my ailments. Anything that is inside my own skin feels private, including my thoughts. After a moment of silence, the doctor said: 'Each of us has a heart, lungs, stomach and intestines. Even though some of your parts are missing.' I started to laugh. I told the doctor about the demons' raucous parties inside my stomach. He did not respond; he turned and took a lidded wooden casket from a shelf. I was terrified, thinking it was a *pao* and that it was my time to go!

From another shelf, the doctor took a bamboo box and poured small granules into a mortar. He crushed many ingredients in the mortar, poured them into a stone container and added liquid from a clay bottle. He mixed and shook and finally filtered the liquid into a smaller clay bottle. 'A spoonful in the morning and evening to exorcise the demons,' he said, then handed me the bottle and bowed. That very same evening, a host of demons exited through my backside with a rumble, smelling of sulphur.

I had already thought about death! When I am dead, the aristocrats' litters will rock along the roads, beasts will carry their burdens, women will draw water from the well, children will make noise, a pig will roast on a spit, the old gatekeeper woman will sweep the gravel pathway, the Emperor will rule, the rain will fall, the flower will bloom and the birds will fly. Everything in the world will be exactly as it was before, even though I am gone. This thought is unbearable.

There ought to be a large hole in the world, a huge pit, in fact, after I am gone. That would tell people that I am missing, that I am not here. Know that, remember that! Fortunately, this morning, I woke up alive.

I sat with Yan Yan once in the gazebo in the garden and watched a plump white cloud sailing above the treetops. It was like a pig blown up by the heavens. The air was almost still, and the cloud was gliding slowly. Suddenly it looked as if the stomach of the cloud had touched a treetop where it would get stuck. 'No, no,' shouted Yan Yan. 'No, no,' I shouted as well. No, no, the cloud slid peacefully above the treetop.

We are sitting at the gambling table, myself and many other old eunuchs. The lanterns cast light and create smoke. We have wine in clay bottles and delicacies on a tray: fried rice cakes, sugared fruit, nuts. The sound of a lute can be heard in the distance. Life could not be better!

One of the players is Lu Hui, who is called The Smiling One. He does not actually smile, but a scar on his face pulls one side of his mouth up. When he plays, his mysterious face gives him an advantage. We old eunuchs play just for fun, but a young eunuch who has almost forced himself at our table does not understand this. He only plays to win, and that is why he always loses. Despite his smile, Lu Hui is a hostile person. I have known him for decades. He hates the earth and sky and everything in between. He hates the Emperor and the court, and he hates the gatekeepers. He is a learned man who has passed the civil service examination, and is able to quote the Master and the Book of Songs and other works. It is rumoured that he even speaks foreign tongues.

I am neither wise nor stupid, though maybe sometimes stupid, but I do not understand his hatred. Perhaps even in his old age he still hates being a eunuch? Perhaps there is an organ inside him that was never cut out? When I tire of Lu Hui's talk, I think that he should start focusing his hatred on his own toes, one at a time. First the big toe of his left foot, then all the others. Same thing with the right foot. Then the left foot again, and so on. He would never run out of things to hate, though he does not seem likely to run out of them as it is.

The shadows dance on the walls, the lanterns reek and the torches stink. The demons are fleeing through my backside, but in the stench of the torches nobody notices.

The Fat One sitting opposite me is a very skinny eunuch named Hong He. Unlike the others, he has a lot of hair. His large eyes glow in his narrow face. In them I can see a reflection of the torch burning on the wall. Hong He talks ceaselessly. He disturbs the other players, but no one tells him to be quiet. Hong He's tongue is so sharp it could sever the artery in the neck.

I know all the lustrous faces around the gambling table. They are my old acquaintances. The people at court often cannot tell us apart because we are eunuchs, not men and women.

At night I walk drunkenly into my cubbyhole. I stumble along the pathway in the yard, stop and raise my head. I can see the stars. In number they are ten thousand times ten thousand.

The bud of a peony is as hard as a pebble. Sometimes the petals will not open, and the bud will wither into a brown ball. Usually when the outer sepals turn, a reluctant bud will bloom into a flower. Gradually the pink, white or bright red petals will start to puff and quiver in the wind. When the whole flower is open like a parasol, one can see its inside. The part that resembles an overturned vase has delicate stems, each with a yellow ball at the end. Golden dust flows out of them.

'I think about death every day,' Li Wei said to me, knocking back his wine. I was amazed. We were young eunuchs, sitting in a warm late summer's evening, drinking wine. We were celebrating in secret. We both worked at the harem. Whereas I was still sweeping floors and dusting, Li Wei had advanced in his career. He was one of those who took care of the harem women's clothes. He was handsome for a eunuch, and women liked him because he was also cheery and playful and his voice was music. 'Why on Earth?' I asked. 'Because I can! Because I am alive! If I were dead, I could not think about death!'

Why do I remember Li Wei? He has been dead for a long time. Do I already know more dead people than living? I can think about death, even though I am seventy years old. I do not want to think about it. I do not want to die while I am still alive!

The large-leafed plants beside the city wall look like stone carvings. One can see all the leaves' veins. From amidst the rosette rises a pale stem with light, violet bellflowers.

I drink wine alone from a gourd bottle in my cubby-hole and become intoxicated. I try to pour wine from the goblet back into the bottle. I almost succeed; only a few drops spill on the floor, but that does not make me any more sober. I lie on my bed. I am a fat eunuch, so I have to drink a lot to get heavily drunk. Thin men get intoxicated easily.

The women at court drink water or tea, but in the villages, women also drink strong rice liquor. A soldier said that drunken women become senseless. They tear off their clothes and stand naked in the rain. I would like to see that. I am not interested in their nudity, but in their madness.

It is raining in cold drops as we old eunuchs sit together in the pavilion drinking wine. The rain becomes heavier; it rustles in the trees and the bamboo thicket. I feel good. I am thinking that someone will soon say: 'It is miserable, it is raining and it is cold.' And someone eventually does, because everybody has an opinion about the weather. Old eunuchs also reminisce about the weather: the terrible summers when the sun scorched the grasses and leaves to ash, the awful winter when snow and ice froze off the branches and the roads were all filled with snow. Everyone can remember some terrible season. People will probably be talking about the weather until the end of the world.

I cannot imagine what people will be like in the future. Perhaps they will be divinely wise, because they have access to the wisdom of centuries and millennia? Lu Hui thinks the people of our time are stupid, lazy, envious, greedy, plotting, power-hungry, treacherous, and violent.

Wong Wu is not here, and I miss him. He is my oldest friend, my best friend. He was sent to accompany the Emperor, even though he is a retired eunuch and cook, because his food is unequalled.

I do not know if one misses a friend in a different way to how lovers miss each other, because they are man and woman.

I do not know what love between a man and a woman is like.

Would I be different in character and knowledge and thoughts if I were a man and not a eunuch? Would I be more quick-witted, more active, more ambitious, more courageous? The other me who was not mutilated is not even a shadow or a reflection in the water to me. Alongside some eunuchs walks the man they could have been, like a twin brother. These eunuchs are angry and bitter. They have been mistreated. They were operated to be unhappy for a lifetime.

I do not know about love the way a man and a woman do. It says in the Book of Songs: *I shall be happy when I meet you. My heart shall be relieved.* Was the man writing about a woman or a friend of his? I do not know.

I know what men and women do when they copulate with one another, but I have never felt the heat or bodily attraction that leads to it.

When I was young I did not like men, because they had ugly voices and rough skin. They were ill-tempered and bossy and mean. And yet, at court, they competed for women's favour, strutting around like cockerels. Men fight, kill, cut each other in half at the waist. They struggle for office, amassing money and land and power. I like women more because I have lived amongst women my whole life. However, there are those amongst them who gossip, plot and organise conspiracies, seeking both power and wealth for themselves and their children.

Eunuchs are not pretty, because they are neither men nor women.

Though now that I am old, I think old people look more or less the same, regardless of gender.

The most miraculous thing about women is that they can grow a child inside them and give birth to it! Underneath the tightly strung fabric is a belly, and inside the belly floats a little human being. A newborn child looks a lot like a pig, and it is not until it is a few months old, or old enough to walk and talk, that it becomes a real person.

I do not know whether small children understand that they are boys or girls. Because they are treated differently, they will learn, at least. Jade figurines and pieces of brick. Even as young men and women, they are the same, thinking only about themselves, their appearance, haircut, and clothing. The mirror is their best friend. Young men look at their reflection just like women do, grooming the hairs of their beards and trying on headwear.

Thinking is an extravagance for which I have time. When I try to recall what I used to think, I cannot remember, and I know not the thoughts of others. I do not know what they are thinking now. When I think about people today, I imagine their thoughts, questions, and answers. It is amusing. I look at the busy people hurrying through the palace courtyard with their skirts fluttering. Their destinations I do not know.

Men know that power makes one a whole head taller. When the clothes are made of thick silk and are fabulously decorated, women will not notice whether the man is fat or thin, wise or stupid, eloquent or inarticulate.

There was a high-ranking official at court who came from a wealthy family. He was a mean, flat-faced man. Yet women cast seducing glances at him. I do not know what happened after he married. I imagine that after taking off his frills he was like a plucked goose. I doubt it mattered, because power, wealth, and titles do not go away when one is naked.

Beauty belongs to rich people regardless of their looks.

The poor people of the villages are ugly because they have lived on scraps, worked their bodies to the bone, and had their skin tanned coarse in the fields. Their hair is matted and they walk crouched. Poverty does to them in youth what ageing does to the rich.

When I see the outline of my shadow on the sand, I think that it is more beautiful than my reflection. My body is rebelling. The night before last, I felt a pain that struck from my hip down into the soles of my feet, as if a hot iron had been thrust through my flesh.

Does a bodily connection between a man and a woman ease pain? Can pain be shared too?

By the palace wall I saw a wrinkled old woman give a toothless smile to a child. The child ran away, even though the woman was holding out a big plum in her hand. Even the animals are afraid of old people. Perhaps they smell death like they do before being slaughtered.

Family is as mysterious to me as the love between a man and a woman. I was a child of my father and mother and had a brother and sisters, but I was cut off from the family a long time ago.

A eunuch has no family. I do have friends, most of all Wong Wu.

Years ago, I accompanied a fat lady in the garden, because she walked laboriously, supported by a cane. A man strolled along the path leading a little boy by the hand. The boy was as sweet as a pear. As the fat lady and the man greeted each other, I realised that the man was the lady's son, and the boy was her grandchild. I stayed behind at a respectful distance and so could not hear the words they spoke, even though the lady's shrill voice usually carried far away. She was scolding her son. I do not know why. She did not even glance at the little boy. The child began to cry. I thought, and felt, that the lady was as heartless as a warlord.

Does reminiscing mean that you once again think, and even speak out loud, your old thoughts? That is how I sometimes feel when I listen to old eunuchs. They nod their bald heads and keep saying 'yes, yes, I remember.'

I do not speak, I only think. Nobody can see inside my head. This I finally believe.

I do not think about the direction I turn in. The Emperor on his throne faces south. I do not listen to good advice, even if it comes out of Wong Wu's mouth.

Because there are many ceremonies, rules, and orders in court, I have feared all my life that I would make a serious mistake, but most of all I have been afraid of wrong thoughts.

Nan Rong taught me in the harem that everything must be done the way it must be done. Mistakes will be punished. He said I would be punished even if I did not realise I had made a mistake. I was a young eunuch and crouched down so that I could be invisible and would not have to do anything. When I thought that I must not think ill, I felt as if my head swelled and grew as big as a pumpkin. Like everyone could see my pumpkin head. For that, I would be punished. I got very feverish. The Old Lady felt my forehead and sent for some medicine. Bitter liquid was poured down my throat. I thought it would explode in my head and spatter my thoughts across the palace's stone floor. When I woke up I still had my head, and the Old Lady was stroking my brow. Even my thoughts were still there.

When I told Yan Yan about the pumpkin head, he said: 'No one can see inside your head, or your stomach, for that matter. No one will even hear when you let air out of your backside.'

Wisdom is a good thing, the Old Lady taught me, but I have come to realise that wit is even better. I do not know if I possess either. Many teachers and officials at court are wise. They know science and the law and the teachings of the Master. The difference between wisdom and wit is that wit does not require wisdom, or learning. It works on its own. Wit grabs things the way a frog catches a fly with its tongue; quickly and skilfully. I imagine a wise frog that ponders deeply what it would mean to catch a fly, what it would require; would it be worth the effort, what would the benefits and the drawbacks be? And how should it be done? By rolling up the tongue, or… That frog would starve to death!

When a wise person dies and is reduced to dust, their head becomes as empty as a duck's egg. The same thing happens to the head of a fool. The wise and the foolish are therefore equals. If one would pause to think about this, one would not bother to learn a single symbol of writing or read a single poem; would not bother about the patterns of stars or study new machines and contraptions. No. That is why I do not think about death.

I am sitting on a bench watching a wagtail hopping on the sand. The bird swings its tail. It looks happy, I think.

Happy! How could I know whether a bird is happy? I am fitting my own mind and thoughts onto animals. I am an animal myself. I wonder what the hierarchy is between animals; is man supposed to be the highest?

When a soldier cuts an enemy's body in half, he leaves the two halves behind and rides off on his horse. I do not even want to remember what sort of animal man can be at his worst.

I feel glad when a frog escapes from the beak of a crane. Am I supposed to be more of a frog than a crane?

One time in the summer, I joined the harem women on a jaunt into the countryside. Wong Wu went along as well, as did many other eunuchs.

The beautiful, lively and cheerful lady Plumblossom, whose real name I will not mention, had for weeks been talking about the wondrousness of nature, and wanted to see the blue mountains, waterfalls and woods for herself. She had read poetry. Usually harem women spent their time in their chambers and walking around the palace garden.

I do not know who gave permission for the outing. Foodstuffs, cookers, and tableware were loaded onto wagons. There were also sweets and nuts in bamboo baskets, and bottles of water, juices, and brewed tea. In their silken pouches, women carried body paints and powders, combs and ribbons. Lutes and flutes had been packed into bags. The equipment also included a tent sewn out of sailcloth, complete with support beams and sleeping pads.

Besides lady Plumblossom, there were five or six young women in the party as well as one elderly lady.

We rocked along cart paths to a mountain outcrop that was considered a place of natural beauty. The women were not wearing silk shoes but heavy, hard-soled wooden shoes. They staggered and swayed as they stepped down from the wagon.

It was beautiful. The grass was short with low,

multicoloured flowers growing on the cliff. A gnarled pine looked exactly the same as in wood carvings. Wong Wu started kindling a fire under the cookers. Three other eunuchs and me set up the tent. Lady Plumblossom ran around in the grass without her shoes, sometimes bending down to smell the flowers. Her friends were sitting on the cliff in a row, like pigeons on a rooftop.

The soup had barely begun to boil on the stove when Lady Plumblossom dejectedly recited the verses of Wang Wei:

> *Lush, lush is the scented grass in the greenness of spring; in the summer's coolness the high pines and mighty willows.*

I understood then that she saw the nature we were looking at as not the right kind! Nature did not satisfy these women's taste.

I walk out of the gate and I feel happy; as happy as a dancing crane, as a goose honking when it flies through the sky!

When I am happy or very sad, it feels as if there is somebody else inside me. A little person. It is not a boy or a girl or a man or a woman. It is I, but in a

71

different manner from the I who walks, eats, belches, sits, and lies down.

A wise friend of mine whose name I shall not mention said and thought things that were dangerous in the realm at the time. He spoke about *qi*, the lifeforce in Taoism. He showed me old wood carvings. Many of them depicted men and women having intercourse. They did not interest me. But in one picture there was a chubby figure; I do not know whether it was male or female. It had an *immortality foetus* inside. It looked the same as the figure within whom it resided.

Even though I am unable to say even to myself how I feel, there is that other within me who feels great joy and sorrow. I am not just a eunuch who is flesh and fat and wrinkling skin; there is an immortality foetus within me. Whatever it might be!

Years ago, Li Wei brought a woman to the eunuchs' party. She had a high haircut in the court style, but her face was dark and rough. She was dressed in bright-coloured silk with large patterns; I cannot remember its colours. I thought that Li Wei must have brought the woman into the palace from outside the walls. Suddenly, she came over to me, grasped my hand, and said: 'Look at how handsome and big you are.' She stared at me for a long time, as if she wanted to suck up my soul. I came close to hitting and pushing her down the steps of the gazebo, though I am usually not irascible. My friends were laughing. I do not know whether they wanted me to get upset or laugh along with them. The woman had mocked me for what I was not: a man.

People may think either the same or different thoughts when they argue about the teachings of the Master or how government should be organised. But can people feel the same emotions? A poem can wrench my heart as if it is talking about me. Sometimes I feel the same way when I am talking with friends. When a man and a woman love one another, do they feel the same feeling? I do not know, because one of them is a man, and the other, a woman.

I am glad that at least inside my head I am alone.

My hip, my ankles, even the soles of my feet are aching! It is wretched! But at least I am not dead yet!

The Old Lady would sit on a seat with a tall back-rest, as her back was aching. The seat cushions had been beautifully embroidered; golden patterns on green silk. She drank tea from a cup, barely wetting her lips. 'When the passion is gone, there is nothing left,' she said. I thought she meant love between a man and a woman. She was not talking about that, but about hatred and lust for power. These are more common in court than love. 'A cowrie shell is considered valuable but is dead on the inside,' she said.

Another time she declared: 'Grieve with me!' I did not understand what she meant. Her only child had died decades ago, and at the mercy of the emperors, she had been allowed to stay at court and in the harem. 'Rejoice with me!' she said. Then I understood and began to laugh. Her first request was easy, the second difficult.

When one of the eunuchs passed his civil service examination, he ran joyfully to tell us who were sitting at a bamboo table about his achievement. I bowed, and so did the others. On that same day, a high-ranking eunuch received a new, finely decorated cloak. When he came to show it to us, everybody bowed several times.

Everything except ageing can be learned, the Old Lady said. She was old when I was young, and now she has been dead for decades. I did not understand what she meant. Perhaps the Old Lady herself was a cesspool of wisdom and not I? Perhaps she was merely repeating ancient wisdoms. I do not know. I do not believe perennial wisdoms any more than I would trust a bird's wing stroke. One can let all kinds of things out of one's mouth, both wise and foolish. Perhaps the greatest follies in the world are more valuable than its wisdoms.

How do the head and body work? Even doctors know preciously little about it. Inside the body are the heart, liver, spleen, lungs, and kidneys. The stomach and its demons, and all the passageways and orifices of the body, are rarely spoken about. No use thinking about it. I do not think about death. Remedies may or may not work. One remedy might help, another might not: different things for different people.

I am sitting outside the Liang gate looking at the river. I can see ships and boats. Everyone is going somewhere. The river flows and the vessels glide by. The current and the winds carry them, but I only sit still. When a bird flies above me, again I have no time to see which bird it was.

Old age starts, the Old Lady said, when one no longer imagines how the future might be different from the present. Personally, I think that old age means imagining one's past to have been different from how it was. Imagining all the things one did not really have, imagining being a landowner, or a high-ranking soldier or civil servant. Do I imagine being a man? I do not. I could have been a scholar, a poet, a painter, or a master of music. I was unable to, or was not allowed to. Thinking of the non-existent, in the past or the future, is pointless dreaming. I am fine with the present, as long as I do not have to die just yet.

The gatekeeper's wife with a jagged chin is sitting on a stone bench. She does not greet me. Her work never ends. She has a stiff back and aching knees, I can see that, but she still bends down to pick up petals one by one. Now, as the chrysanthemums are shedding their leaves in the wind, she sinks into despair.

I am lying in the hay looking at the sky. It is blue and clear from one edge to the other. I fall asleep, and when I open my eyes again, the clouds are beginning to cover up the sky. Thin, curly clouds are rising from the edges like carded wool. The woolly ribbons are moving slowly, drawing together. I stare at the sky and the clouds. Slowly, the ribbons get tangled with each other, and little by little, the sky begins to look uniformly grey. I have witnessed it all happen. I am old. I am alone. I do not want anyone to look at me.

I do not want to be alone. I want to play games with my eunuch friends and drink wine. When it was hot in August, we sat in the gazebo. Sweat trickled from our foreheads to chins and down along the neck onto the stomach and bellybutton. The wine was thick and sweet and I drank too much of it. In the game, I wanted to win all my companions' paper money and copper coins. I wanted to beat Li Wei for his books. I challenged him to a game of dice, but he refused. I said that he was a stupid old eunuch! He said that I, Wang Wei, was older, poorer, and more stupid. Because I was too drunk and am too kind and clumsy and old, I felt like grabbing him by the throat, but did not have the energy.

Talking is often pointless. That is what I think, as if I were a great wise man. A thick fog is hanging above the field. The treeline cannot be seen. Then I encounter a friend, and my mouth starts churning like a bean mill.

To those who believe in omens and forecasts, a good prediction should be written down afterwards. That way, their life would feel worth living even in their old age.

Man is just a sack of rice, Yen Wu told me. He was an old eunuch when I was young. We sat on the same cart on our way to some skirmish. I understood only later what he meant. He wanted to say that man lives inside his skin that is like a sack, and that he stuffs rice inside it to stay alive. He did not believe man to have any more value than that. I am old now, though I do not think the same way.

Fate, or the world, or its events, are cruel. My brother died when he was seven years old. Still, I do not have an opinion about the entire world.

A heart without love is harder than a plum stone. I think about the lady and her grandchild in the garden. No shoot from a heart like that could grow into a tree. But what are feelings, really? At court they are often sour belches or releases of air from the backside!

I have wanted to feel lightness and joy, but sometimes my fat body has weighed too much. My aching bones and stiff joints are no longer fit for dancing, though I still twirl around in my mind.

I wash my face and groom my hair. I still have a little left on my head. Each morning I do the same. Each morning. In the evening I wash my face again. It feels like morning was only a moment ago, and I have to do these things all over again. Time has grown shorter. A day is merely a breath, even a year is just a sigh. When I was young, it felt like next spring would never come.

A poor, thin woman is standing outside the palace wall with her vending cart. I see her often. I have been encountering her for decades. She too is old now. Her hair is white, her neck crooked.

She sells vegetables, fruit, and flowers, depending on the season. In the autumn, I have purchased roasted almonds and preserved pears from her. I now buy some sugar-coated lotus blossoms from her. Although her face is so wrinkled that it is hard to tell her expression, I can see that she is sad. I do not know why. I do not ask; I do not say anything. Her sadness nevertheless makes me sad.

I do not want to think about death. Why should I think about it? Pouring rain, a typhoon and a snowstorm are hard to predict, but death is certain. Thinking will not change that.

The aching of the bones and pain in the stomach are different. I cannot stop thinking about them, because they are constantly speaking inside my body.

Death is a scimitar strike through the torso. Head and shoulders here, stomach and legs there.

I am shivering on a stone bench. I am so scared that I am freezing. I see a sword blade pointing towards my chest. I shake and think of Wong Wu; who knows where he is? He will not have time to help. I close my eyes. The sun is growing dim.

With my eyes closed, I see my death only from within, not from without. The body grows tense preparing for the moment of death. The spirit leaves, and I am no more. I do not even have time to feel pain. I wait. I open my eyes. A ray of sun hits my eye. The stone feels rough under my bottom. I am not dead.

I do not know why I did not die after all. Many friends are already dead. I am no better or worse than they. Before his death, Yan Yan asked: 'Why does everyone die?' He meant himself and his friends. He answered himself: 'Because everyone dies.'

He was right, but that is a wisdom I do not need.

Yan Yan and Wong Wu liked to talk about the teachings of the Master. I dared not say out loud that I thought his creed was too fond of order and commandments. I once said to Wong Wu that the Master has harnessed all the horses, but the wild ones are still galloping on the steppe. Wong Wu replied: 'How will goods be shipped if horses are not harnessed?' I thought for a moment and replied: 'By wheelbarrow.'

Last spring one eunuch died. He was fifty years old when it happened, and he had lived in a wild way, even though he was a eunuch. He was a clay bottle filled with rage. His fury was not directed at enemies like it is with soldiers, but at himself. When he was young, he worked as a helper in the palace kitchen. He chopped vegetables. When the cook's assistant scolded him for being too slow, he chopped off the fingers of his left hand. His little eyes burned with black fire. Many were afraid of him, but I never was. He was a gentle person. When he found a plum stone on a gravel pathway, he planted it in the ground. He loved cranes and other birds. He would sit on top of the wall watching as the birds flew overhead during migration time. He never hurt anybody other than himself. Once we drank ourselves to inebriation together. Our tongues were slurring, and when we against our sensibility spoke about important persons at court, their names got twisted in strange ways. We sat on the bench with a wine jug between us and laughed until we fell off. Because of his wild nature he was transferred to a far-away corner of the realm. I never saw him again.

I do not want anybody to die.

Yu Geng began to feel ill a year ago. He had trouble breathing. He was wheezing like a soaked pair of bellows. He was too weak to join us at the gambling table. Later he became too weak to even come to the dining table. We other old eunuchs took turns bringing him drink and soup, even though he did not want anything, not even water.

I sat at Yu Geng's bedside in his cubbyhole and felt uncomfortable. Yu Geng was a wise man. He reminisced about the time he had studied for his civil service examination. He reminisced about the machines he had helped make. The finest of them was a clock powered by water. He loved wisdom, but above all, he loved knowledge. He read and studied his books to the last moment. He never spoke about death. He probably thought it was a natural phenomenon that applies to every living being except himself. I do not think he was afraid of death. He was probably astonished when it came.

Joy and excitement fill my mind when I realise that I am not dead yet. Dying is sad, because then there will be no more life. The joy is so great that it is too big for the heart, the head, or the lungs! It is almost as if I was dying purely for the joy of being able to live.

Compared to death, old age is merely melancholy. Who am I, who was I? Who even cares? Perhaps I was a human, a eunuch, a heron, a snail, a frog, a duck, a palace dog, perhaps just the droppings left by a palace dog? Old age pushes you across the boundary, whether you are the Emperor or just a lowly eunuch! An old person is no threat to anyone, and no one wants to ally with one who has been sentenced to death.

On their deathbed, everyone wants to think that they lived a good life. Life may have been hard, poor, and miserable. So why live at all? Death is still worse than even the most miserable life.

Humility in the face of death is pointless, or at least toadying is. If you look down as you beg, you will not even notice when someone gives you something.

The only advantage of old age is the ability to think, even when the body refuses to obey. The mind can disappear from the body in young or old age.

I had a terrible dream, or was it a vision? It must have been a dream, because I woke up. I saw a grey, thin, creeping character who came in through the door of my room. The room was the cubbyhole where I sleep. I jumped up from my mattress and tried to shout in a loud voice. Only a wheeze came out of my mouth. I flailed with my arms to scare away the creature. My throat had closed up. Finally the figure turned and slipped out of the doorway like a shadow. That was when I woke up. My body was shaking; I was covered in sweat. I was alive and happy.

III

I am sad. Wong Wu came back from his trip, but he is ill.

His face is growing thin and his belly is shrinking. He does not know what is wrong with him, and neither does the doctor. The doctor has examined his heartbeat and felt his liver, but he could not find a reason and the remedies have not helped.

Wong Wu sits on the bed in the infirmary with his hands on his lap. His bald head is frail and spotty. The eyes look large in his narrow face. His gaze is clear and empty like that of a small child. I talk to him casually. I try to bring a smile to his face, but he does not smile. Whenever somebody drops a heavy object in the hallway, Wong Wu is startled. He hears but does not listen. It feels heavy for me to stay. It feels as if I am talking to a stone.

Since Wong Wu is not a high-ranking official, the doctor does not treat him particularly respectfully. I feel like yelling that everyone should respect a good cook.

I do not want Wong Wu to die, because he is my best friend. My only friend.

Years ago he got angry at me. Did not want to talk, turned his back when we ran into each other. I had said that he was greedy and cheats at gambling to win coins. I cannot remember how long he was upset with me. We made up. I wondered then what the line of inheritance was for eunuchs. Who would inherit his fortune, or mine? That does not interest me now.

I want Wong Wu to get better so that I can tell him what a fool he is. I want to tell him how much I like him. In my vase is a white chrysanthemum and another one with yellow petals inside the white petals. I intend to give them to him.

Wong Wu will get better, and we shall both live another ten thousand times ten thousand years!

If I could, I would jump, run and dash back and forth along the hallways, flap the skirts of those in power, yell, laugh, tell everyone what I think about our current Emperor, what I think about all emperors, major landowners, and officials, what I think about the redistribution of the administration, what I think, how I think.

I sit on a stone bench by the wall, and the sunshine is gone. I can feel the rain in the air, though not a single drop has fallen.

Acknowledgements

The author would like to thank Markku Eskelinen and Professor Lauri Paltemaa.

Biographies

Kristina Carlson (b. 1949) is a Finnish writer. Her work has won the Finlandia Prize in 1999, the State Prize in Literature, the 'Tack för boken' medal, and the English translation of *Mr Darwin's Gardener* was longlisted for the DUBLIN literary Award. Both *Mr Darwin's Gardener* and *Eunuch* were nominated for the Nordic Council Literature Prize.

Mikko Alapuro is a literary translator and philologist working between Finnish and English.

Graphic design by Dorte Limkilde
Typeset in Songti TC and Bembo Infant
Printed and bound by TJ Books, United Kingdom, 2023

The translation of this book received funding
from the Jenny and Antti Wihuri Foundation

Lolli Editions gratefully acknowledges the financial
support of FILI – Finnish Literature Exchange,
and the Fondation Jan Michalski

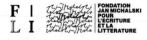

A CIP catalogue record for this book
is available from the British Library

ISBN 978-1-915267-12-2

Lolli Editions
New Wing, 88
Somerset House, Strand
London WC2R 1LA
United Kingdom
lollieditions.com